SHADOW BATTLE

SHADOWS OF THE VOID BOOK 9

J.J. GREEN

BOOKS ORDER

The Books of Shadows of the Void - Complete Series

Prequel: Starbound
Book 1: Generation
Book 2: Stranded
Book 3: Dawn
Book 4: Shadowrise
Book 5: Underworld
Book 6: Burned
Book 7: Trapped
Book 8: Mars Born
Book 9: Shadow Battle
Book 10: Shadow War
Books 1 - 3 The Galathea Chronicles
Books 4 - 7 The Earth Chronicles
Books 8 - 10 The Galactic Chronicles

1

———

They'd been waiting for longer than an hour in the cold, bare meeting room at Ganymede Outpost for the Transgalactic Council officers to arrive. Jas rubbed her arms and tried for the hundredth time to find a comfortable position on her hard plastic chair.

"I thought *they'd* be waiting for *us*," she said to no one in particular. "Why did they tell us to meet them here if they weren't here already, or nearby? If they set out from halfway across the galaxy after they sent their message, we could be waiting for days, or weeks."

The rest of the crew of the starship *Bricoleur* were ranged around the room. Carl, the pilot, had given up on attempting to fit his lanky frame into the too-small seats, and was leaning against a wall, his arms folded across his chest. A bulge around his middle was the sleeping form of his alien friend, Flux, inside his shirt.

"They won't be coming by ship," he said. "Council staff travel by Transgalactic Gateway. It's instant."

"Is it?" Jas had heard of Transgalactic Gateways, but she didn't know much about them. Their use was restricted to

Council business only and the technology was a well-kept secret. "So how come they're taking so long?"

"Krat knows," Phelan Lee, captain of the *Bricoleur*, muttered.

Next to him, his sister, Sayen, yawned. Jas envied the woman's skin augmentation, which made her impervious to air temperature extremes. There was no way Jas could feel sleepy in that icy room. Though the government station at Ganymede Outpost had been built deep beneath the surface of the frozen moon, she'd detected little increase in warmth during the long descent by elevator.

Jas had also detected a little frostiness in the official who had met them on their arrival. It had caused her to wonder if Shadows had infiltrated the facility, but it seemed safe enough for the time being. Jas speculated that it might be living in freezing conditions that had made the Ganymede staff stand-offish.

"Well I've had just about enough of this," exclaimed Dr. Sparks, rising from his seat. "I'm exhausted. I'm going to ask where our quarters are so I can get some sleep."

"You can't," said Sayen. "You know all the important information about the Paths. You have to be here for the meeting."

"I don't think it'll matter too much if I slip off for a while," replied the doctor. "As Jas said, it could be hours until the Council officers arrive. It's been a long, harrowing day and I can't keep my eyes open a moment longer. Someone can come and get me if they want to talk to me."

"Don't go," said Sayen. "If we have to find you and bring you back here, it'll waste time."

As Dr. Sparks and Sayen bickered back and forth, Jas frowned. She'd never liked the doctor and the more she got to know him the colder her feelings grew. Not only was he a bigot, but despite the efforts she and others had made to rescue him from his informal imprisonment on a Martian scientific research station, he hadn't yet expressed any gratitude to them nor any sorrow about the alien empath who had died to save his life.

Sparks said, "It doesn't matter what you say, I simply have to rest. Just send someone for me when the officers arrive." He went over to the door, but when he opened it, the Ganymede official who had greeted them at their arrival was outside. She drew back, her eyebrows rising at the sight of Sparks.

"Um...the Council managers are here," she said. "They're on their way over. Could you move some chairs and tables back to make room for them?"

The woman indicated the furniture in the half of the room nearest the door. Jas wondered how large the creatures were.

They stacked chairs and tables in the corner while the Ganymede official stood at the open door watching the corridor. Her face broke into a smile as the Council officers presumably approached, though her smile was actually more like a grimace.

Jas sat down once more as scratching sounds from outside signaled the officers' imminent appearance. The odor of vanilla invaded the room.

As the first officer appeared through the door, Jas sat up in her seat. She'd encountered many aliens during her career in deep space security, but nothing compared to what she was seeing then, not even in her worst nightmares. Coated in a bronze exoskeleton and walking on ten pairs of articulated legs, the Transgalactic Council officer was massive and insectoid. On either side of its head were two huge compound eyes, and it had sharp mandibles for a mouth.

The alien was followed into the room by another of the same species, though this one was a little larger at around two and a half meters tall and wide. The third to enter the room was larger still, and its carapace was golden. The vanilla scent they gave off was strong and threaded with spicy undertones.

"We apologize for keeping you waiting," said the golden alien. "We had some urgent matters to address before we left." Subtle flowery aromas wafted across the room. Jas wondered if the creatures used their pheromones to communicate.

"I'll be back in a little while," the Ganymede official said before leaving them alone to talk.

Jas had battled long and hard and many people had died and been injured to get word to the Transgalactic Council that Earth was being invaded by Shadows right under the nose of its government. Her hard, uncomfortable seat was forgotten as she leaned forward to hear what the Council was going to do to help her fellow humans.

"Firstly, we must introduce ourselves," the golden one went on. "My English name is Martha, and my colleagues are Rahul and Peter."

As the humans also introduced themselves, Sayen sent Jas a sidelong smile. The aliens' appearances were certainly at odds with their mundane names.

"For reasons I will explain shortly," Martha went on, "we do not have much time. The message we received from you about the invasion of Earth was short, and we require more information. If one of you could briefly outline your first encounter with the organisms you call Shadows and the related events up until you arrived here, we would be most grateful."

The others turned their eyes to Jas. She was the one who had first discovered the existence of the Shadows on a far distant planet what felt like a very long time ago. She took a breath. She didn't know how she was going to tell the Council officers everything that had happened over the last few months *briefly*, but she began to speak.

As simply and concisely as she could, she narrated the important incidents, like the fight aboard the prospecting ship, the *Galathea*, the battle on the colony world, Dawn, and their encounters with Shadows on Earth as they attempted to inform the Council about the invasion.

The officers were silent throughout her story, though judging by the aromas that drifted around the room, they were speaking with each other as they listened. Sayen, Carl, and even Dr. Sparks added in extra points as Jas spoke.

When she related their re-encounter with the Paths on Mars, Rahul interrupted her. "Pardon me, but may I ask where these Paths are at the moment?"

"They're aboard my ship's shuttle in the docking bay on the surface," Phelan replied.

"I see," Rahul said. "It seems to me that, according to what you told us about finding these creatures within a Shadow trap but unaffected, they are extremely significant. We must speak with them urgently. They may be the breakthrough we've been looking for. Their information may give us an advantage in the battle."

"Battle?" Sayen asked.

"Yes," Martha replied, "we are about to engage militarily with these dreadful invaders. Regarding your story, we had thought that Earth had so far evaded attack, but apparently we were wrong. I would like to thank you for everything you've told us. Your information is most useful. I will record the coordinates of the planets you mention before we leave. Now, we have only a short time remaining, and I must use it to explain the galactic situation with the Shadows."

The creature settled down on its many legs.

"The Transgalactic Council first became aware of these invaders several Earth years ago, though it took some time for us to understand the nature of the menace. At first, it appeared that hostilities between galactic civilizations were increasing. Throughout the galaxy's history, there has never been a time it was entirely at peace, but attacks and invasions were the highest they'd been for a long time. Our military arm, the Unity, stepped in as a peacekeeping force wherever possible, but its resources were stretched thin by the numerous conflicts.

"It was not until we were alerted to thousands of individuals who claimed that their family members, friends, and colleagues had been taken over by unseen forces that we began to suspect that these aggressions were not exactly as they seemed. Our investigations also revealed the presence of Shadow traps on many worlds that were in conflict with other civilizations. The coincidences mounted up.

"Further investigations continued, and as soon as the realization dawned as to what was actually happening, we responded. So far, we've identified hundreds of planets that the Shadows have taken over. The Unity, together with the military forces of so-far unaffected planets, are attempting to destroy the invaders and rescue surviving citizens. We have reclaimed some worlds, but for every planet we free from the Shadows, another two appear in its place. As we speak, the Unity is on the verge of yet another battle. We came here directly from a meeting to finalize the battle plan."

"But what about Earth?" Jas asked. "What are you going to do to help the people of Earth?"

"According to the information you supplied," Martha replied, "we are in no doubt that Earth is indeed in the midst of a Shadow invasion, but I am afraid that your world is one of many civilizations in need of our aid. We cannot do anything immediately, but when the Council can spare the resources, we will do all we can to help."

"What?" Jas exclaimed. She thought of Erielle and Makey, her friends who had returned to Earth intending to fight the Shadows there. Were they even still alive? How long would they have to wait before help arrived? She stood up. "That's not good enough. Earth needs help *now*."

Carl said, "Jas, I don't think—"

"No, Carl," she said. "This is wrong." She swung around to the aliens. "Why do you think we went through so much to contact you? Earth's a Council ally, isn't it? Humans are entitled to its protection. People are dying as we speak. You have to help us."

The Council officers didn't reply immediately. Scents of warm chocolate and acetone filled the air as they talked among themselves.

Martha said, "We understand your position and we sympathize with Earth's plight. Be assured that we will do everything in our power to fulfill our obligations to come to its defense as soon as we are able. But at the moment we simply cannot. A massive fleet of ships controlled by Shadows is currently approaching a highly strategic region of the galaxy. Every vessel at the Unity's disposal has been amassed to stop them. If the Unity prevails in the ensuing battle without heavy losses, we may be able to dispatch a force to address the situation on Earth."

Carl straightened up from his position leaning against the wall. "Is it too late to join the battle?"

"I'm not sure," Martha said. "I doubt that engagement with the enemy has commenced yet. Why? Do you wish to fight?"

Carl said, "I'd like to, especially if it means Earth might receive help quicker. I'm a pilot."

"What?" Jas exclaimed. "Wait a minute."

"Do you have combat experience?" Martha asked.

"Yes," Carl replied.

"There may still be time for you to take part in the battle if you leave now," Martha said. "We can open a Gateway to the Unity recruitment point. I'm sure the officers would be happy to see a trained combat pilot. There is a scarcity of them."

"No," Jas said. "Carl, don't go."

2

The Transgalactic Gateway opened in the meeting room. Though it was Jas's first time seeing one, she was too distracted by Carl's imminent departure to take much notice. It had all happened so quickly.

He avoided her pleading gaze as the green mist that heralded the Gateway began to form.

"Carl," Jas said. "please don't go. It's too soon. We've only just arrived from Mars. You need to rest up. It's too dangerous."

He only glanced at her and shook his head slightly, as if telling her not to interfere.

"All right, I'll come with you then," Jas blurted. "I'll fight too. I'm sure the Unity can find something for me to do."

"I am afraid that we need you here for the moment," Martha said. "We need further information on the Paths. Sadly, I do not think this battle will be the last. I am sure there will be many more opportunities to fight the Shadows in the future. For now, you can be the most useful to us by telling us more about the Paths."

Jas was numb. It had been only hours before that she

and Carl had kissed for the first time after a growing close-
ness between them that had lasted weeks. She hadn't imagined that he would be snatched away from her—that he
would *choose* to leave her—so soon.

"Carl, please," she murmured, her heart tearing in two.
Phelan, Sayen, and Dr. Sparks looked away, embarrassed.

The green mist had coalesced and began to lazily swirl
into a spiral.

Finally, Carl turned to her. His face grave, he stepped
over and touched her upper arm. "I'm sorry, Jas. I have to do
this. The Shadows killed my parents. I have to fight them."

"Please prepare to step through the Gateway," said
Martha. "It will be open for only a few seconds."

"Don't worry about me," Carl said. "I'll be back as soon
as it's over." He kissed her briefly and returned to his position in front of the whirling mist.

The ache in Jas's chest was unbearable. A thousand
words rose to her mind and were dismissed. She couldn't
speak as she struggled to understand why Carl had to leave
her. Maybe if she'd had a family, she tried to tell herself, she
would do the same. But she had no family. She only had him.

The scene blurred before her eyes. She didn't see the
moment when Carl stepped into the mist. She only heard
the others' quiet goodbyes. By the time she wiped her vision
clear, he was gone.

After a moment or two, Jas realized that Martha was
talking to her.

She swallowed. "What did you say?" she asked the alien.

"I said, I would like to see these Paths. I know of approxi-
mately two thousand and seven hundred sentient species
who live in our galaxy, yet I have never heard of anything
that matches your description. And according to what you

have told us, these creatures have extensive knowledge of the Shadows."

Jas was still too upset to say more, which Phelan seemed to notice, for he answered in her place. "If y'all want, Jas and I can go collect them from my shuttle."

"That would be most convenient," Martha said.

"Come on," Phelan said to Jas. "Give me a hand."

Leaving the meeting room and returning to the elevator that would take them up to the surface proved enough of a distraction to calm Jas down a little, which had no doubt been Phelan's intention. In spite of his brash, slightly insensitive demeanor, Sayen's brother was as warm-hearted as his sibling.

The two of them stepped through the bare metal elevator doors and stood side by side as they began to ascend. Phelan's hands were clasped behind his back and his eyes were focused ahead. "Looks like we'll all be joining in a Shadow battle soon enough."

Jas nodded. "I think you're right."

"I would have volunteered too," said Phelan, "but I wouldn't have had any idea what I was doing. I've only ever captained the *Bricoleur* on mining expeditions. I've never been in combat."

"I'm pretty sure neither has Carl."

"What?" Phelan turned to her. "Then why did he say he had?"

She shrugged. "So they'd let him go fight, I guess."

"Krat. Well, I'm sure he'll be fine anyway. He's a damn good pilot."

"He is." Ever since she'd known him, Carl had always flown expertly. Jas recalled how he'd saved the lives of the crew of the *Galathea* by crash-landing the starship onto K.

67092d and later lifting off from the planet's surface. But the best pilot in the galaxy could still be shot down.

They were at the top of the elevator shaft. The doors opened, revealing the walkway that led to the docking bay and the *Bricoleur's* shuttle. Now that Carl had gone, Jas wondered how they would return to Phelan's ship, which was in orbit above Ganymede occupied only by the android navigator, Prosper.

She looked out of the walkway windows on each side. It was always daytime on tidally locked Ganymede. Jupiter was reflecting the Sun's rays onto the moon's frozen wastes. The icy expanse that surrounded them reminded Jas of her college days on Antarctica.

"You okay? You look like you're gonna faint." Phelan was looking at her, worried.

She took a deep breath and exhaled, releasing the memory of the time someone else had left her abruptly and without warning. "I'm okay. Let's get these Paths. The sooner the Council figure out what they can tell us, the sooner we can all move on."

Phelan opened the airlock and they went inside the small shuttle. The Paths were, unsurprisingly, exactly where they'd left them. They so closely resembled large bag-shaped fungi, it was hard to believe that it was only through their enigmatic activities at the Valles Marineris Spaceport that Jas, Sayen, and Sparks had escaped Mars.

Jas's mood lifted as they approached the Paths. Though she knew her feelings were influenced by emotions radiating from the empathic aliens and were a reflection of their reaction to her appearance, she was glad of the effect.

She and Phelan gathered up the brown sacks. Their arms full, they returned to the waiting Transgalactic Council officers.

3

Dr. Sparks had explained his experiences with the Paths in detail to the officers by the time Jas and Phelan returned with them. Jas hoped that the officers were telepathic and could speak with the aliens, but after a lengthy pheromone exchange, Rahul announced that this was not the case.

"We appear to only sense their emotions," he said. "It is most frustrating. These creatures do not appear to be very skilled at telepathic communication."

"Flahive didn't seem to have much trouble speaking with them," Sayen said. "In fact, he said they were so loud he had to ask them to whisper."

"You have a companion who is able to communicate with these beings?" Martha asked.

"Had," said Jas. "He was killed on Mars."

"Oh dear," said Rahul. "That is sad and most unfortunate for us. May I ask where this person originated?"

"He was Cruthian," Phelan replied. "He was my engineer. The *Bricoleur* has an Oootoon engine."

"Ah yes," Rahul said. "Everything becomes clear now.

High-gravity planets such as Cruth tend to promote the evolution of exceptional telepathic talent." The insectoid alien waggled his head, causing his antennae to wave around. More odors emanated from the Council officers as they continued their discussion in silence.

Jas had been standing since she and Phelan brought the Paths to the meeting room, but suddenly exhaustion threatened to overwhelm her, and she sat down. It seemed that every muscle in her body was aching.

The Council officers began questioning Dr. Sparks about the Paths once more, but Jas barely listened to the conversation. Memories of Carl occupied her thoughts. She remembered the happy-go-lucky co-pilot of the *Galathea*, the tetchy friend on Dawn, his sleeping form at her place on Earth, him driving Ozment's truck. How long would it be before she would see him again? How would she find him among the thousands of pilots fighting in the Shadow battle?

Sayen interjected loudly into the Council officers' conversation with Sparks, telling them they needed to hear what Flahive had told them in the bar after meeting the Paths but before the doctor had caught up with them. The pheromones of the Council officers faded as Sayen related almost word for word what Flahive had told them about the Paths existing in another realm outside the physical universe, and how the Shadows also existed there.

"This is truly remarkable. Incredible, in fact," exclaimed Peter. "What you are telling us is the stuff of mythological tales and beliefs. We simply must find out more. These Paths may not only be our key to defeating the Shadows, they may enlighten our understanding of the very nature of existence itself."

"Look," Jas said to the aliens. "That might be true, but I

don't think we can tell you any more than we already have. What happens now? Are you taking the Paths with you? Can I join in the fight against the Shadows? I was a security chief aboard a starship."

"If you do not mind waiting a few more hours," said Peter, "I would like to—"

"I do mind," said Jas. "Whether the Paths have secrets to the universe to reveal or not isn't relevant to us. We've told you about what's happening on Earth and we've brought the Paths to you. There isn't anything else we can do. It's past time that we went into battle."

"Now wait a minute," Sparks said. "Speak for yourself. I'd be very happy to help the officers for a while longer."

"You would," said Jas.

"Jas," said Sayen, frowning.

"Please, please," said Martha. "Do not argue. We wish to resolve the question of what the Paths can tell us as quickly as you do. Unfortunately, the high-gravity civilizations where empaths who could speak with the Paths live are within the section of the galaxy currently controlled by Shadows. Though we could open a Gateway to one of those planets to try to recruit an individual to help us, the likelihood that we would encounter a Shadow is high. We must find another way to communicate with them. But I have an idea."

Once more, the Council officers exuded odors as they talked among themselves.

"For krat's sake," Jas said in an undertone to Sayen after a short while. "How much longer do you think they're going to keep us here?"

Before Sayen could reply, Martha spoke. "We would like to try something that could be a little dangerous. I am afraid that our physiology prevents us from performing this experiment ourselves, but we believe a human would be highly effective."

"What? What are you talking about?" Jas asked. Her patience had entirely dissipated and any effort at civility had gone with it.

"You are familiar with the equipment the Council uses to test the presence of Shadows?" Rahul asked.

"You mean Shadow scanners?" said Jas. "Yes. I already told you that we stole one from a spaceport. What have they got to do with this?"

"Our fight against the Shadows was greatly aided when we discovered the one difference that distinguished them from their victims," Peter said. "A Council operative who was coated in invisibility spray—a human invention, I believe—saw an aura around Shadows that no other things living nor inanimate exhibited. Through a series of experiments, we discovered that it was the tiny amount of mythranil included in the invisibility spray that enabled the wearer to identify Shadows in this way. Using this knowledge, we incorporated similar trace amounts of mythranil into prototype Shadow scanners and found this made them foolproof at detecting the Shadows' auras."

At Peter's revelation, Jas's mind flew back to what Carl had said when they rescued Sayen from the Shadow holdout in Antarctica. He'd mentioned seeing that same aura. "So, what are you saying?" she asked. "I still don't get how that's going to help you find out more about the Paths."

"We are, of course," continued Peter, "perfectly aware of the illegal uses and effects of this powerful narcotic. It sends the user into a euphoric, trance-like state lasting several hours."

Sparks, who had been sitting in a corner of the room, his chin resting on his hand, apparently thoroughly bored now that the conversation had turned from him, suddenly gasped and stood up. His eyes popping, he pointed a trembling finger at the Paths. "I understand," he exclaimed. "I know what you mean. Of course. Of course. It makes perfect sense. That was where I went. That was where they sent me."

"What are you babbling about, Sparks?" Jas asked.

"When the Paths are threatened, they defend themselves by sending the thing threatening them to another place mentally," the doctor replied. "The body remains, but the mind of the attacker has departed. The place they send their attacker's mind is the place the Paths come from. The effect is to make the threat go away temporarily. If they feel sufficiently threatened, they send their attacker away permanently, and the attacker dies. I see it now."

"Does anyone here have the faintest idea what he's talking about?" asked Jas. "And if so, could they please explain it to me?"

"I think I understand," said Sayen. "The Paths have no physical power here, but their mental power is strong. They can control our minds and transfer them to another plane, where the Paths and the Shadows come from. But I don't understand the connection with myth."

"Let me explain," Martha said. "The narcotic mythranil is well known for its ability to transfer the mind of the user to another place, figuratively speaking. But from what we now understand about how the trace presence of myth in an observer of a Shadow confers the ability to see their aura, we can speculate that the drug's effect is not figurative, but literal. The user mentally travels outside the physical universe to the realm where the Paths and Shadows exist."

"So..." said Sayen. "You're thinking if someone goes to

this place, they could connect with the Paths on their home territory?"

"That is indeed our conjecture," Martha said.

"Sorry," said Sparks, "I'm not threatening them again. It's out of the question. Besides, I don't remember noticing anything resembling the Paths while I was in my trance."

"It would be foolish for the Paths to approach a threat within their own domain," Rahul replied. "But we are not proposing that anyone threatens them. That would be unethical. We have a different method in mind, but unfortunately we are unable to do this ourselves. We require a human volunteer."

"I'll do it," Jas said. Whatever it was, she didn't care. Nothing seemed to matter much anymore.

"Excellent," Martha said. "We will send for the mythranil immediately."

4
_____

The conjoined Shadow minds rippled as their thoughts spread out across the Void. More and more victims in the physical realm had wandered or been driven into traps, and more Shadow replicants were created and crossed over. The small trickle of movement had become a flood.

In the place where spacetime existed, mental contact between Shadows remained difficult. There, they were confined to solid bodies, separated from each other and shaped by—haunted by—the memories and personalities of their victims, which they retained from the copied brain matter and coding of their cell structures.

Their numbers had grown so great that extensive coordination was vital, now more than ever. This need had been identified and was being addressed as they moved toward the final stage of their plan: domination. When spacetime prevented efficient contact, they used the technological communication systems of the beings they had destroyed. It brought great pleasure to the Shadows to operate the marvelous contraptions of the physical plane, especially the vessels that carried solid bodies from place to place. They had gathered a great number of these. The battle was upon them, and they could use the vessels to good effect.

On worlds where the Shadow presence was sufficiently large, they had seized control of the planet and hastened the destruction of the remaining sentient beings. Among other civilizations, where their numbers were yet inferior, the Shadows bided their time. They had strategized their victim selection so that, though Shadows were not the majority on these worlds, they held key positions within powerful organizations. When the battle was won, these planets would also fall under the weight of the victorious invaders, undermined from within.

The alliance led by the Transgalactic Council had vastly underestimated the extent of the Shadow presence. It would have a surprise waiting when the worlds it was supposedly defending rose up against it; when the friends they did not suspect turned upon them. But until the right moment, the Shadows had to operate carefully.

Meanwhile, though the physical realm was falling quickly under their attack, opposition within the Void was growing stronger. It was inevitable. Their presence was reduced as more and more Shadows split from the fusion and crossed over to the other side, while the might of their Void opponents remained the same, immensely strong and fighting the Shadows' efforts at every turn.

When a few parts of the opposition had managed to slip through and emerge in a trap, the Shadows had feared that they would also have to fight them on the physical plane. But there, the opponents were weak and ineffectual. Though the Shadows could not force them to return to the

Void, they did not have anything to fear from them in the physical universe.

Unlike the victims the Shadows took. *They* had much to fear.

5

"Don't do it, Jas," Sayen said. She'd caught up to her friend at a Ganymede Outpost airlock. Jas was already wearing an environment suit and she was getting ready to go outside.

Jas lifted the visor of her helmet. "Huh? I'm only going for a walk. I hate being cooped up in here with nothing to do while we wait for the myth to arrive."

"That isn't what I meant," said Sayen. "You shouldn't take that drug. You've never done it before. Some people die when they take that stuff. You don't know what could happen. What if they get the dosage wrong?"

Jas shrugged. "Someone has to take it. If the Council officers are right, I might be able to find out the Shadows' weaknesses."

"Then let me do it," Sayen said. "My augmented body's more robust than yours. I can probably tolerate the myth better."

Jas shook her head. "Phelan has already lost both his parents. It isn't fair that he should risk losing you too. I don't have anyone who'd be too bothered to lose me."

"That isn't true, Jas, and you know it."

"Isn't it?"

"Of course not. Phelan and I couldn't bear to lose you, but more than that, what about Carl?"

"What *about* Carl?" Jas's gaze turned to the wintry landscape through the airlock window. "I thought he cared about me, but he didn't hesitate to leave me when he had the chance. I guess I was wrong about him."

"Oh, Jas." Sayen sighed.

"I'll be outside for a while," Jas said. "Could you tell them to radio me when the myth arrives?" She snapped her visor closed and pressed the airlock's inner door.

"Wait," Sayen exclaimed, but the door slid into position and Jas turned her back while waiting for the atmosphere exchange to take place.

Sayen hadn't donned an environment suit in years, not since her safety training to become a deep space navigator. By the time she'd zipped up and snapped everything into place and passed through the airlock herself, Jas's long legs had already carried her more than a hundred meters away from the station. Sayen hailed her friend over the radio, and Jas paused and turned. She waited as Sayen made her way carefully over the frozen ground, strewn with ice boulders. In the low gravity, she found she could bound over the ground quite quickly.

Jupiter hung threateningly in the sky above, its bands of color interspersed with angry swirls as massive storms tore through its atmosphere. The gas giant's presence was so close, Ganymede seemed constantly about to fall into it, inexorably drawn into the gravity well. Sayen shivered, though her suit's heating was making her feel toasty compared to the chilly station. She withdrew her gaze from the moon's overbearing master as she reached Jas.

"It's a bit much, isn't it?" came Jas's voice over her radio.

Sayen could barely see her friend's lips move through her darkened visor.

"Jupiter?" she replied. "Yeah, just a little."

"It reminds me of K. 98352g. Do you remember? Only there it was the system's sun that took up most of the sky."

"I remember the planet but not the view. I never used to go down to the surface in those days."

"Oh yeah. That's right," said Jas. "You didn't like to, did you? You told me once that while you were on a prospecting mission, you used to pretend you could step aboard the shuttle and go right down to Earth if you wanted."

Sayen chuckled. "Did I say that? It was true. I did used to pretend I was only a shuttle ride from Earth." Sayen swung around to view the desolate gray-white, cratered scenery that stretched monotonously to the horizon. "Were you headed somewhere in particular?"

Jas's laugh sounded in Sayen's helmet and she saw the ghost of her friend's wry smile. "No. Nowhere in particular. Want to come along?"

"I was hoping for the invitation," Sayen replied. As they set off, she imagined how they must look: Jas inside an environment suit large enough for a tall man, and herself, slim and petite, toddling and bouncing alongside her. They crossed the barren ground, passing eons-old ice rocks for a while in silence.

"You know, Jas, I feel like such an idiot," Sayen said.

"Huh? How come?"

"Those Council officers...I think I met some of their species not long ago. I keep thinking that if I'd said something to them at the time about the Shadows invading Earth, maybe it would have saved us a lot of trouble. Some people might still be alive."

"You met those aliens before? How'd you manage that? It couldn't have been on a prospecting mission."

"No, it wasn't. Do you remember when we went to steal the Shadow scanner from the spaceport? With Ozment?"

"Yeah, of course I do."

"We stopped at a park in the mountains overnight. Erielle was still weak and in a lot of pain from the wounds on her legs. I couldn't sleep, and I went for a walk. I ran into some of those creatures."

"You did? I don't remember you saying anything about it."

"There was so much going on, and I was worried sick about Erielle...and I didn't think it was important. But maybe if I'd told those tourists what we knew..."

"No, don't beat yourself up, Sayen. Just because they're the same species, that doesn't mean the ones you met had any connection to the Council. They probably wouldn't have had any idea what you were talking about."

"Yeah, maybe. I hope so," said Sayen, then, after a moment, "Jas."

"What?"

"You don't really think that Carl doesn't care about you, do you?"

Her friend sighed. "I didn't think so when we left Mars. Now, I just don't know. The minute the Council officers made him the offer to leave, he took it. Like he realized he'd made a big mistake."

"But he wanted to go fight. He wanted to take part in the battle with the Shadows. He's risking his life."

"That's what I mean. He's risking his life just to get away from me."

"Krat, Jas," Sayen exclaimed. She could hardly believe

what she was hearing. "What's wrong with you? Are you sick or something? This isn't like you."

"No, I'm not sick. I don't know what you mean."

"You don't know what I mean? What I mean is, where's all this self-pity coming from? You sound like a kratting teenager. Of course Carl cares about you. You *know* that. You spent the last several months avoiding the fact and pushing him away, but you know it as sure as we're standing here."

Jas didn't reply for a moment, then she asked, "So how come he left me?"

Sayen heard an uncharacteristic tremble in her friend's voice. "Jas, I guess I know how you feel. Erielle left me too, remember? And I was just as hurt and angry as you are right now. But she had to go to fight the Shadows on Earth and protect her people. And it's the same for Carl. The Council mentioned the opportunity, and he took his chance. He had to do it, the same as Erielle and Makey did. He probably thought he couldn't live with himself if he didn't try to avenge the deaths of his parents."

"You didn't go," Jas said.

"I wasn't as quick off the mark as Carl, but I will, Jas, I will, when the time comes. I'll never forget what the Shadows did to Mamma and Daddy."

Without a word, Jas set off walking again.

"Wait a minute," Sayen said, hurrying to catch up.

Jas went determinedly on, continuing to say nothing. Sayen glanced back at the lonely steel tower and squat base that marked the entrance to the underground outpost. The station had grown smaller as they'd increased their distance. Though her suit's navigation would lead them straight back to it, the dwindling image made her uneasy.

"Don't you think we should turn back?" Sayen asked. "The myth should be here soon, and rad levels are high on

Ganymede. We probably shouldn't stay outside more than half an hour or so."

Jas's breathy sigh came over her radio, followed by, "I'm being really dumb, aren't I?"

"You mean about Carl? Well..." Sayen considered how to put her response kindly, but she knew that Jas could take the truth without offense. "Yeah, you're being real dumb. Can we go back now?"

Jas about-faced and began to stride back to the outpost. Sayen trotted along behind her.

"You know, Jas," she said. "I don't think Carl went to fight in the Shadow battle just for his parents' sake. I think he wants to beat the Shadows because he wants a peaceful future for both of you."

"Really?" Her friend's voice was high and quavering once more.

"Yeah. When we were aboard the *Bricoleur* before we went to Mars, he came to my cabin—to cheer me up I think. I was pretty low for a while after Erielle left. He brought that daft animal with him. We talked a little, and he did make me feel a bit better. Then we got to talking about everything that had gone on."

She paused. "I probably shouldn't tell you this, but Carl cares about you so much, Jas. He told me so. He was all confused at the time we spoke because he thought you two were close, but you always pulled away if anything started to happen. Yet you'd been so free and easy with that officer on Dawn. He couldn't understand why you were so reluctant to be with him, but now that he knows he's important to you, I'm sure he wants to fight for you too."

"He compared my feelings for Idris with my feelings for him?" Jas exclaimed.

"I guess he did. It's natural, isn't it? But it's okay now, right? Because you finally decided you want to be with him."

Jas stopped in her tracks, almost causing Sayen to collide with her. "This is terrible. He's got it all wrong. I didn't hesitate because I didn't like him as much as I liked Idris. I hesitated because…Krat. Now he's gone, and I can't explain why I acted like I did. Sayen, this is awful. What am I going to do?"

Sayen wasn't exactly sure what Jas was upset about, but she tried to reassure her friend all the way back to the airlock. Her efforts didn't seem to do much good. When they were inside and Jas had removed her helmet, Sayen could see her friend remained worried and distracted. It was too late for them to talk more, however, because the myth had arrived.

6

———

Jas had rarely felt as bad as she did at that moment. She was naked and lying under a blanket in the Ganymede Outpost's medical center, waiting to receive the mythranil that might or might not send her to the place the Paths came from. But she didn't feel bad because she feared what was about to happen. More than becoming addicted to the powerful narcotic, more than getting lost in that place beyond the physical universe, more than dying, in fact, she feared never having the opportunity to set Carl straight about what he meant to her.

Ever since the trauma she'd experienced when she'd been at training college in Antarctica, she'd had a certain approach to relationships. She hadn't shied away from them entirely, but when someone was interested in her, she was always careful to keep everything light and easy. She preferred dating on missions when the man was planetside, knowing that, in a few days or weeks, circumstances would force them to part company, usually amicably, after a brief fling. She'd always steered clear of dating shipmates, who she would be unable to avoid until the mission's end, which could be months or sometimes even years in the future.

With Carl, everything had been different. For the first time since she was eighteen, Jas had felt out of control of what was happening to her. Though she couldn't have put her finger on the moment when Carl had become something more to her than just her pilot friend and shipmate, she knew that her feelings were serious, and her vulnerability had scared her.

On Dawn, with Idris, things had progressed as usual up until the Shadow invasion. The lieutenant had been a good person, but Jas wouldn't have thought twice about him six months after departing the colony. Her feelings for Carl, by contrast, were for life. In the past, she'd lost someone who'd meant that much to her. She didn't think she could survive that loss again, so it had taken a long time for her to let her true feelings show.

"Are you ready?" Martha had come in while Jas was lost in her thoughts. The alien's golden head with its shining compound eyes appeared above her. In the claws at the end of one of her front legs she held a hypodermic needle filled with a deep crimson liquid. Her claws looked almost as sharp as the inner mandibles of her mouth, which protruded as she spoke.

"Um, I think so," Jas said.

"I can assure you that I will hit exactly the right spot," said Martha. "Though my species' vision is not as effective as human's, at this distance I can detect the odor profile of your body. The points of sensitivity are clear to me. I will inject the mythranil in the area that gives the greatest effect. The Council is extremely grateful to you for participating in this experiment."

Dr. Sparks entered the room, rubbing his hands

together. "I'll do it," he said cheerfully. He seemed to have caught up on his sleep while they'd been waiting for the myth. But still, Jas thought, the massive insectoid alien with razor-sharp mandibles would be a preferable alternative to the doctor.

He took the hypodermic needle that the alien handed him.

"As you wish," Martha said. "I am sure that you are a competent physician. It really does not matter, providing that Ms. Harrington begins the experience and gathers any useful information as quickly as possible."

The Paths had been placed in a corner of the room in case their proximity might create some kind of beneficial effect. Jas's gaze lingered on their brown, baggy forms as Sparks lifted the blanket.

"You do know what you're doing, don't you?" she asked the doctor.

"Of course I do. Tut tut. Such little faith. As a matter of fact, mystical medical theory is one of my specialties. I took additional credits in it. I know all the meridians and adjacent neural structures. Never fear."

She rolled her eyes. She'd always known the man was a quack. But in this case he did seem to be the right person for the job.

"As a matter of fact, I quite envy you," the doctor went on. "If the effects of myth are similar to the trance the Paths put me in during my little sojourn on Mars, you're in for a delightful experience. Now, please remain still. I've found the exact spot."

Jas gasped as a bright point of pain materialized to the right of her groin. She clenched her teeth, fighting the urge to leap up and rip the hypodermic from Sparks's fingers. Myth was supposed to be a narcotic—a relaxing, pleasurable, doped-up experience. Jas hadn't imagined she would have to endure agony to receive a dose.

But in another moment, the pain was replaced by bliss.

Jas wasn't sure if her eyes were closed or open, but she could feel as much as see an infinite expanse surrounding her. She was floating in infinity, and she was part of it, endless and unconfined. Whirls of colors she did and didn't recognize spun around her, though she was also a part of them. She was empty and she was whole; she was split into a billion pieces and she was complete. All her desires and needs, worries and fears, were gone. Existence was all and it was perfect. *She* was perfect and free.

She floated forever, but at the very edge of her mind something nibbled. Like a grain of dust in her eye, a tiny piece of gravel in her shoe, an invisible scrap of food stuck between her teeth. It was the sense of a task incomplete. Something she had to do or see, or someone she'd left behind. The tiny speck of irritation marred the perfection. Jas mentally pushed at the thing, willing it to disappear. But it resolutely popped back. No matter how hard she tried, she couldn't escape it.

A disruption appeared in the ever-evolving patterns that surrounded her, and she understood that she was not alone. The colors churned faster, until, "Welcome," a chorus of voices echoed in her mind. The sounds seemed to bathe her in cool waters and enveloped her in such feelings of security and warmth that she forgot to answer.

The voices repeated their greeting, calling Jas to a modicum of concentration. "Hello? Who's there? Who are you?" she asked without speaking.

"We are the creatures you call Paths in the physical realm."

Jas could vaguely remember something related to that name, but she no longer cared about anything. The name's significance slipped from her mind like raindrops through cobblestones.

"Human, you must listen."

Why wouldn't they be quiet? There was that speck of irritation again, niggling at her. "What? Why?" She tried to move away from the beings who spoke, but they were all around her and all through her too.

"Human, we wish to help you, but you must hear us."

Jas couldn't escape the voices. Wearily, she replied, though her voice was also no more than a resonance in her mind. "What do you want to tell me?"

"You are in the Void, and entities from here are invading your plane of existence. They are leaving here for your universe and destroying living things there. We want to stop them. We want to help you."

The relevance of their words still escaped Jas.

They continued, "We do not want the others to continue to leave and take away the brief, time-bound lives of beings on the physical plane."

Concentrating with all her might, Jas said, "I don't understand. Why do these others want to leave here? Everything is perfect."

"Objects from your plane flit in and out of existence here. They notice these things and desire them. They lust for the complex creations that you physical beings use to move across distances. Here, they have no need of them, for there are no distances. Every point is simultaneously connected. So they must move to the physical plane to enjoy them."

Jas's mind began to drift. She couldn't grasp what the things were telling her. She began to relax once more into elation and bliss.

"Human, please listen. Because we do not wish to destroy and replicate a physical life form, we are all but helpless within your realm and cannot exist there indefinitely. You must take this information back with you. Many of the others have left the Void. We believe they spread throughout your realm, much farther than you imagine. We have read the minds of those remaining here and learned that if your side appear to be winning the battle with them, the others will reveal themselves and betray those closest to them. Your defense will fail. You must take this information back with you and warn your kind of the danger."

But Jas couldn't properly understand what they were telling her. Words were gossamer in the Void.

7

Jas didn't know how long she'd been floating in the Void. Time didn't seem to exist. She'd always been there, and she'd never been there. She could no longer hear the beings. Only a trace of their warning remained in her mind. What had they been referring to? She couldn't remember. It didn't matter anyway.

A moment or a millennium later, she became aware of more entities. Had the original beings returned? Maybe they would tell her their message again.

But these things were not the same. A wave of unease coursed through her. They didn't embody the bliss of the Void. They were its opposite values—negativity, confinement, emptiness. Jas tried to move away from the things, but the dimensionless place offered no escape. Tendrils of fear wriggled into her, invading her joyful bliss.

"We know you," voices said. "Those of us on the other side encountered you there. You have ended our existences. You cannot return to the physical plane to destroy more of our kind. You must stay here. We will keep you here."

The writhing tendrils of fear hardened within Jas,

sparking flames of pain. Her mind was brought rapidly into focus. Where was she? What was happening? What were these things she could perceive but not see?

She struggled, her mind a mess of fear. The things that held her tightened their grip. All Jas's years of training kicked in and she tried to fight, but she had no body. She tried to scream, but she had no mouth. Without eyes, she couldn't see her attackers. She could only feel them. She was trapped.

But like the rays of a gentle dawn over the waves of a stormy sea, Jas felt the first beings return. The initial reaction of those that held her was to tremble as the strength of their resolve weakened. The powerful grip that held her slackened.

Then a discordant tone sounded. The things holding Jas squeezed her tighter. Her mind was being crushed. The sensation was agonizing.

All around, a battle broke out as the opposites fought. Colors flashed and disappeared. Voices erupted and were silenced. Jas was lost in a sea of turmoil, and ever the grip of the things that held her grew tighter. The first beings were trying to free her, but the ones that held her were too strong. Ever tighter they gripped. They were squeezing her from existence. They were...

The sensation lessened and transformed to a rocking motion. She was being pushed from side to side roughly. She began to slip from the entities holding her. She was fading away. One last attempt was made to grasp her, but she was gone.

Someone was pushing her. Why was someone pushing her? She heard voices in the far distance. They were familiar voices, and for the first time in what felt like forever, they were coming from outside her head.

"Jas, can you hear me?" It was Sayen.

"It's okay. She's coming out of it now." Sparks.

"Thank krat for that." Phelan.

She opened her eyes. All three familiar faces were hanging over her.

"M' okay," she mumbled. "I'm okay. Quit crowding me."

As they backed off, Jas shakily sat upright on the narrow cot, pulling her blanket over her shoulders. She shivered. Martha's head was poking in at the doorway.

"You've been under for hours." Sayen said. "We thought you were never going to come around. How are you feeling?"

"I'll check you over," Sparks said. "If everyone could leave?"

"Really, I'm okay," said Jas, and for the most part, she felt she was. Except that she was very, very down. She wanted nothing more than to return to the place she'd left. She could see how easy it was to become addicted to myth.

"Did you find out anything?" Phelan asked.

Jas rubbed her face with her hands. "About what?"

Martha squeezed a little more of her bulk into the room. "Could you tell us if you found out anything about the Shadows or the Paths?"

"The Shadows or the...? I know the names..." Exactly what they were, she wasn't completely sure.

"Have you forgotten the nature of the experiment you undertook?" Martha asked.

"Jas, what can you remember?" asked Sayen.

Trickles of memory ran into her mind. She began to recall snippets of things that had happened recently and people she'd met. Erielle. Makey. The Shadows.

"Just give me a minute, will you?" she said. She shut her eyes, trying to remember. Gradually, the last few months came back to her. She remembered what had happened and the reason for her disorientation. Like opening a barely healing wound, she recalled that Carl had left.

"Are you sure you're all right?" Sayen asked.

"I'm afraid I have to ask everyone to leave so I can conduct a thorough medical checkup," said Sparks.

"I'm fine," Jas snapped.

"I apologize for hurrying you," Martha said, "but time is of the essence. If you have anything to tell me about your experience while under the influence of the mythranil, now would be the appropriate time."

"Ough." Jas put her face in her hands.

"Jas, what's wrong?" asked Sayen.

"I can't remember," Jas replied. "I think I met some beings, and they told me something. There were also some other things that were trying to keep me there, and a fight. And then I was back here. But that's it. Everything else is just a few memories of the run. I've no idea if I met the Paths, and if I did, I have no idea what they told me."

"Ah, I see," said Martha. "That is disappointing. No doubt an effect of the drug. However, several doses remain. Though it is probably now too late for any information we glean to help in the current Shadow battle, we could find out something to be used in the future. Perhaps we can try again."

"I don't think it's going to help," Jas said.

"That may or may not be the case," said Martha. "We will never know unless we try."

"I really don't think there's a lot of point," said Jas. "Look." She pointed to the corner of the medical center were the Paths had been placed. It was empty. The Paths had gone.

8

———

Sleeping wasn't easy for Jas at the Ganymede Outpost. A chill penetrated from the surrounding rock ice that the station's inadequate heating system couldn't dispell, and the government-issue bedding was no compensation. Earth's Global Government clearly hadn't spent much funding on the station. To them, it must have been only a handy strategic spot in case of an attack from outside the Solar System. The Government had claimed the place, left its stamp, and then forgotten about it.

But it was more than the cold that was keeping Jas awake that night. Every time she closed her eyes she felt disoriented, as if she were floating in zero-g. Her Martian childhood and long years of visiting other planets had accustomed her to sleeping in gravity lower or higher than Earth's, so she knew it wasn't Ganymede's weak gravity that was causing the dizziness. She guessed the sensation was an after-effect of the myth.

She could hardly remember anything of the *run*, as it was called. Mostly all she could remember was a sense of perfect peace and happiness—joy, even. She could see how hard it would be to resist taking another dose of the illegal narcotic, and another, until the desire for myth became all-consuming. Yet she knew that there was something, or rather *someone*, who stood in the way of that ever happening to her. Happy or sad, she didn't want to leave her reality behind while there was still a possibility of being reunited with him.

Pulling her coverlet over her shoulders, she turned on her side, closed her eyes and tried to go to sleep. But her feet were icy. Her cover was too short for her long body. She pulled up her knees, turned onto her other side and tried once more to sleep. Finally, she drifted into a doze.

Behind her eyelids, colors began to shift and swirl. The sensation of floating returned, but Jas was so tired that she managed to ignore it and slipped farther toward uncon-sciousness. The shapeless, unmoving sack bodies of the Paths appeared in her mind. Only they were no longer motionless. They were moving, spinning around her. Then, the colors behind them began to darken, and a sense of dread crept up on Jas.

The darkness felt significant, though in her fogged mind, she didn't know why. The Paths' movements became agitated, as if they wanted to leave but lacked sufficient physical control. The colors continued to deepen until they were almost black. Jas shared the Paths' fear, but there wasn't anything she could do about it. Her body refused to obey her mind, and she was forced to remain still. Her mouth moved, but her vocal cords would not create any sound.

As well as deepening their hues, the colors—nearly black by then—seemed to encroach. Something terrible was about to happen, and there was nothing Jas could do about it. Suddenly, the darkness was upon the Paths. Jas struggled against invisible bonds to help them, but in a moment they were gone, devoured by the pitch black cloud.

With horror, she realized the cloud had turned its attention to her.

At last, Jas's body responded to her mind's pleas, her bonds snapped, and she sat up abruptly, hitting her head on the low overhang. She gasped and winced, putting her hand to her brow.

What had *that* been about? she wondered. Then some of the content of her encounter with the beings in her run began to filter through to her. She couldn't remember exactly what they'd said, or even if they'd said anything at all, but she remembered the essence of their meaning. She finally understood that the benevolent beings had been Paths, and that they'd been trying to tell her something important.

Jas leapt up and ran barefoot into the corridor. She hammered on the door to Sayen's room, which was next to her own, forgetting that there was a door chime.

"Sayen, wake up! We have to contact the Council. We have to warn them."

After a moment, the door slid open. Sayen was sitting up in her bunk in the darkened room, her cropped blonde hair sticking up at the back. As she turned on the light and smoothed down her hair, Jas went in and repeated herself, adding, "The Paths told me during my run that there are Shadows on both sides of the battle, and if we seem to be winning the Shadows are going to reveal themselves and turn on their shipmates."

"Krat. Are you sure? How do you know? How come you didn't remember earlier?"

"I don't know. It was probably the myth addling my

brain. This all came to me just now as I was falling asleep. We have to contact the Council and warn them. Sayen, what about Carl? What if his copilot is a Shadow?"

"Okay, okay. You're right. We have to tell the Council."

Martha and the other Council officers had returned to wherever they'd come from to continue their work while the humans got some much-needed rest. They'd said it was too early to decide what to do with the humans as they hadn't given up hope that a myth run might still yield information about the Shadows.

Sayen swung her legs down and got up. Together, they ran to the operations room of the station, which was staffed by a corpulent administrator Jas hadn't seen before. As they went inside, the man took his feet off his desk and leaned forward, his belly hanging between his knees. "Hey, you aren't supposed to be here."

"We have to contact the Council immediately," Jas said. "Please, open a line to the one called Martha, who was here today."

"Can't do that," the man said. "You have to get permission, and you won't for a line. It's too expensive. I can send a packet if you go through the proper channels."

"No, this is urgent," said Jas. "We need a direct line."

"No way. It's not happening. Do you know how much energy that takes? Nearly as much as the station produces. It's out of the question. What's this about, anyway? Nothing could be that urgent. The Council was only here a couple of hours ago."

"There's no time to argue," exclaimed Jas. She approached the man, her tall frame towering over him. "Open a line."

The administrator's thick neck bent back as he looked up fearfully at the Martian.

"Jas, it's okay," Sayen said, pulling her friend away from the daunted man. "Sir, it's a matter of life and death, not just for humans, but for the entire galaxy. Please, open a line."

The man rubbed his neck and looked from the red-haired Martian to her diminutive friend. "Well, that's a bit different, isn't it? Why didn't you tell me that in the first place? I'll just contact the—"

"You'll contact the Council officers who were here today," said Jas. "Now."

Shaking his head, the man activated his interface with a swipe of his fingertips and pressed the screen in several places. He hesitated and glanced at Jas's towering figure before giving a final prod. The station's lights dimmed.

"Told you this would take us to capacity," he said. "I hope your message really is as important as you make out or you'll get me into a lot of trouble."

Above the screen, a hologram of the golden head of Martha appeared. Her mouthparts were moving, but no sound was coming out.

"Whoops," the administrator said, and he pressed the screen again.

"We appear to be having a communication problem," said Martha. "Could you please repeat your message?"

"The Paths told me there are Shadows on both sides," blurted Jas. "Both sides of the battle. I couldn't remember after my run, but it came to me just now. I'm sure it's true. Please, tell the Unity commanders immediately."

"You are positive?" Martha asked. "Humans dream, do they not? Are you sure that this is not a product of your imagination, filling in gaps in your memory?"

"I'm certain of it. Please, please tell them."

"The battle has been progressing for some time, and

there has been no sign of what you say, but, very well, I will pass on your message with all haste."

"Thank you," said Jas. "And one more thing. I want to be there too. I want to take part. Please let me fight in the battle, because I think it's far from over."

9

Sayen and Phelan were saying a tearful goodbye, and Jas stood with her back toward them, trying not to intrude. She was facing the bare wall of the meeting room, where Martha had said she would open a Gateway. The Council had agreed to Jas's request to join the reinforcements preparing to join the battle with the Shadows. Her background in security smoothed her way. They'd also accepted Sayen on the basis of her space navigation skills and her modified body. But untrained personnel like Phelan, Martha had said, were better off defending their home planets, where their knowledge of the local environment and population was invaluable.

Phelan had argued that Sayen should return to Earth with him aboard the *Bricoleur*. The pain and indecision in Sayen's eyes was clear to see, but in the end she'd decided to fight the bigger fight, saying that her ability to navigate across space was more useful to the galactic effort. Dr. Sparks had elected to take his chances waiting things out on Ganymede.

At one time, Jas would have been glad that she didn't

have those ties that were so painful to sever, but in her case that was no longer true. In fact, she was guiltily aware that her drive to join the Shadow battle had less to do with her desire to help defeat them—though that was important to her too—and more to do with her need to find Carl.

Sayen came over and stood beside her as the green motes sparked into existence in the air in front of them. Jas had already said goodbye to Phelan, but she glanced over her shoulder for a final farewell. Sayen's brother was leaving the room, his head and shoulders bowed.

The Ganymede Outpost had arranged for a pilot to fly the *Bricoleur* to Earth. Now that the Global Government had been forced to officially acknowledge the Shadow presence, military forces had been mobilized to repel the invasion. Though it had annoyed her mightily at the time, Jas hoped that she would see Phelan throwing his baseball at the ceiling over and over again at some point in the future.

Neither Jas nor Sayen were taking anything with them to the Unity reinforcements rendezvous point. They *had* nothing to take but the clothes they'd printed aboard the *Bricoleur*. The green dust of the Gateway began to coalesce. Jas shivered. She would be glad to leave Ganymede Outpost behind, for more than one reason.

"Did you recognize the name of the place that Martha mentioned when she agreed to let us fight in the battle?" she asked Sayen.

"Yeah, I've heard of it."

"Is it hot there?"

"As hot as they want to make it, I guess," Sayen replied. The Gateway spun faster.

"Huh? They have climate control?" Jas asked.

"Aboard the *Camaradon*? Of course."

"Aboard? I thought we were going to a planet. You mean it's a—"

"Step through now," came a voice from the other side of the Gateway.

Jas walked into the green swirls. She could see nothing but emerald light. One of her feet seemed to step onto nothing, and then she was through. Her other foot hit a hard, scuffed metal floor.

"Keep walking," barked a voice. "Out of the way. Move it."

Jas withdrew her gaze from the distant walls and ceiling, myriad of shuttles, and plentiful groups of aliens, closed her gaping mouth and did as she was told. She walked through an archway scanner and past a Unity soldier who was reading the scanner results on an interface. She turned her attention to the massive starship shuttle bay the Gateway had brought her to.

Sayen appeared behind her, and together they went in the direction indicated by the Unity soldier manning the exit. As they went toward a line of waiting aliens, Jas looked over her shoulder at the Gateway. More creatures from around the galaxy were stepping through and following them as ordered by the soldier.

"Move up," instructed the creature who was monitoring the end of the line. At the front was another alien, checking an interface. They stood patiently at the end of the line of new recruits. Jas hadn't seen such a range of galactic life all in one place before. Her attention was also taken by their surroundings.

The bay was bigger than anything she'd ever seen. It was bigger than any starship she'd ever worked aboard, in fact. Thirty or forty huge shuttlecraft of a military type were parked down each side. These vessels had no fancy decorations or frills. They were utilitarian craft, not designed to impress with their looks. Several of the shuttles bore the marks of attacks. Repair crews were at work fixing the damage, roughly patching the holes and replacing scorched and melted areas of metal.

Elsewhere in the bay, teams of new recruits were being allocated weapons and put through hasty drills. The Gateway Jas and Sayen had traveled through closed, and the last of the newcomers walked, slid, or hopped to the end of the line.

"It's quite something, isn't it?" Sayen said, her gaze also roving the massive room. "Biggest ship in the Unity fleet, I heard."

"You knew about this ship?" asked Jas.

"Gee, don't you ever watch the vidnews?"

"Step up," said the soldier processing the recruits. They'd reached the front of the line.

"Name, origin, and background," the alien said. It was a quadruped with two prehensile pincers on either side of double orifices in its head. Around its neck hung what seemed to be a translator, for its voice broadcast from the device. The soldier held an interface in its pincers.

It repeated, "Name, origin, and—"

"Jas Harrington from Earth. I worked as chief of security on prospecting starships. I want to speak to someone in authority."

"Chief of security? Good. We can certainly use you. Ever commanded defense units?"

"Yes, but—"

"Even better. Go to the corner of the bay next to the doors to the take-off zone and ask for Lieutenant Yeroch. He has a squadron of units and no idea what to do with them. Here. Take this." It handed her a device similar to the one hanging from its neck. The alien turned to Sayen. "You. Name, origin and—"

"Wait," Jas said. "I have to speak to someone in authority right away." She looked over the alien's head to other figures in uniform moving around the bay, but she didn't know which rank the symbols on their uniforms indicated.

"Top right corner of the bay," said the alien. "That's an order, soldier."

"Jas," said Sayen, "we told the Council what the Paths said. Let them deal with it."

The alien repeated to Sayen, "You. Name, origin, and background."

Jas set off as instructed. Sayen was probably right. The Council would tell the Unity of the potential danger. No one here was likely to take her seriously anyway. She was just another recruit. But whatever happened, she was surely going to keep a close eye on everyone around her.

It was a long walk to the corner of the bay. When Jas looked back at the line of recruits, she saw that everyone had disappeared. She wondered where Sayen had been sent, and with a lurch of her stomach she realized that, like Carl, her friend was also on her way to a dangerous fight. Only with Sayen, she hadn't even said goodbye.

Whoever was in charge of the defense units was clearly having a hard time controlling them. On her way to her destination, she came across several units wandering around aimlessly and getting in the way of the repair crews. She told them to follow her, and the part-organic androids dutifully marched along behind her.

By the time she arrived at the corner of the bay, Jas had collected seven units of varying models and specs. Another group of the towering androids was standing together as she approached, and she spotted an amorphous creature made of a transparent jelly-like substance among them. All the creature's internal organs were visible, including the inner structures of its four eyes, which on the surface looked disconcertingly human.

"What are you doing with my defense units?" the creature screeched. A regular human voice had broadcast the words in an even tone from its translator, but the life form's own high-toned speech almost overwhelmed the English. Jas wasn't sure if it was as angry as it sounded or if that was just how it talked.

"I found them roaming around while I was on my way here," she replied. "I thought I should bring them with me as they don't seem to know what they're supposed to be doing."

"How did you make them obey you?" screeched Lieutenant Yeroch.

Jas replied, puzzled, "I just...told them what to do."

"Huh, they won't do anything I tell them. I commanded them to wait around for a while until we found them a leader, and half of them walked off."

"They did what you told them to," said Jas. "You instructed them to wait around, so they did that as well as they could. If you want them to wait here, you have to tell them exactly that. They do just exactly what you tell them."

"Is that so?" The creature's voice became so high-pitched, Jas winced. "If you're so good at it, you can take over. They're all yours."

10

O ver the next couple hours, Jas inspected the defense units and got them working as a team. Some were Earth-manufactured and their organic components were human cells, which seemed to make them easier for her to manage. Others were kinds she didn't recognize, and she had to be even more careful than usual to simplify her language to make her meaning completely clear.

Working with such a mismatched bunch wasn't going to be easy, but the tasks her squadron had been tentatively assigned were at least straightforward: defend the starship from boarders and sweep captured vessels for pockets of resistance.

After checking their integrated weaponry and asking for a status report from each unit, Jas repeated marching orders to accustom them to moving together in a predictable, orderly fashion. This wasn't easy for the units, given their range of sizes and shapes. She was grateful that they all seemed to have organic neural networks that enhanced their adaptability and learning powers.

A few of the units reminded her of the AX models she'd commanded on Polestar prospecting missions. She'd even checked their chest plates, feeling a kind of nostalgia for the times when her life had been much simpler and she only had a myth-addicted, greedy captain to deal with.

She remembered the time she'd snuck aboard a shuttle to try to check out a Shadow trap planet after she'd been confined to quarters. Carl had been the shuttle's pilot, and she recalled him finding her hiding in the hold, along with unit AX10.

She sighed. None of the units under her command were AXs, and she didn't know where in the galaxy Carl was.

Jas came out of her reverie almost too late, as the defense units were about to march directly into a shuttle. "Right turn," she said. As one group, they turned. Jas gave a small smile of satisfaction. Even the smallest of them, LK29, who she'd mentally nicknamed Pint-Size, was finally keeping up.

"Put this on," said a voice behind her, making Jas jump. The words had been accompanied by a screech. She turned to find Lieutenant Yeroch handing her an armored suit and helmet. She took the suit and held it up. It seemed roughly the right size.

"You're shipping out in fifteen minutes. Transport 17," Yeroch continued. "You've been assigned to the destroyer, *Infineon*.

"Are we losing the battle?" she asked.

"No," Yeroch replied. "The word is, we're on the verge of victory, though we've incurred heavy losses. They're calling for reinforcements for the final stage. You've been assigned to a human majority ship." He left, repeating, "Fifteen minutes. Transport 17."

WHAT JAS HAD THOUGHT WERE shuttles were actually military transports with starjump capabilities, she realized. Hence their size. She also realized that the scars they bore were from attacks as they carried troops to and from starships taking part in the battle.

The defense units climbed inside Transport 17, their feet clanking on the metal floor. The interior had definitely seen better days. Inside were two long benches on either side of the long, low cabin. The floor sloped slightly, down to a central channel that led to a drain, no doubt to carry away the stomach contents of new recruits unused to starjumping. The channel didn't look like it had been cleaned any time recently, and the smell of the place confirmed the fact.

Bare pipes encrusted with grime ran across the walls. Dirt also dimmed the light shining from square panels in the ceiling. The corner of Jas's mouth lifted as she imagined Sayen's reaction to traveling aboard the Unity's transportation.

The defense units spaced themselves out evenly along the benches, and Jas took the spot closest to the exit. The hatch closed and sealed itself. They were left in silence and dimness. The defense units looked sinister in the half light, but Jas wasn't too bothered about being alone with them. It had been weeks since she'd worked with androids, and she finally felt she was on familiar ground.

Still, her stomach was in knots. It wasn't that she was afraid of fighting in the battle. It was hardly the first time she'd been in combat, though this would be her first military excursion. Her memory of the Paths' message was making her nervous. If undiscovered Shadows on the Unity side were going to turn against their shipmates, now would be the time.

The Shadows had managed another infiltration unsuspected. Jas guessed that it must have taken place long before the Council discovered the invasion. The Unity had scanned her and the other volunteers immediately when they'd arrived on the *Camaradon*, but if Shadows were already on the inside, it didn't matter. The Unity's precautionary strategies were too late, and now, in the heat of battle, it couldn't possibly check all its personnel.

Had the Council made it clear to the Unity that it faced danger from within its own ranks? She had no way of finding out from her lowly position as a new recruit, and she was cut off from contact with any of the Council officers who had come to Ganymede.

At least the Shadows only replicated organic organisms, Jas reflected. She had nothing to fear from her units, but the minute she set foot aboard the *Infineon,* she had to suspect everyone she met.

The transport lurched as the pilot maneuvered it to the take-off pad, ready to fly the vessel to a safe distance from the *Camaradon* before starjumping. Jas told the defense units to fasten their safety harnesses, and she did the same. She slotted her helmet into place and snapped the visor closed, not knowing what to expect when they arrived at their destination. The cooled, purified air that puffed into her helmet was a welcome change from the stench and stuffiness of the cabin.

"LK29, do we have comm?" she asked.

"Affirmative, Corporal Harrington."

Jas had memorized all the units' designations, and she went through her list, checking that she was in contact with each one individually and as a team.

As she finished her check, the pilot's voice came over her helmet's comm. "Jumping in thirty seconds."

Vibrations juddered through her bones as the transport's engine generated power. The vibrations increased until they were almost unbearable. The Unity clearly didn't waste creds on their troops' comfort. Jas set her teeth and gripped her harness tightly. Just when she thought she couldn't bear the reverberations any longer, they jumped.

11

As they emerged from the jump, the floor of the transport seemed to drop away. For the first split second, Jas thought it was an effect of the jump, but it soon became apparent it was more than that. She was forced abruptly downward, which caused her internal organs to crush into her diaphragm. She grimaced and waited for the pilot to correct their rapid drop, except he didn't. The transport continued to accelerate in the same direction. The pilot must have spotted something as soon as they'd come out of the jump, Jas realized, and he was maneuvering to avoid it.

Jas guessed they must have emerged into the middle of a firefight, but she didn't want to distract the pilot by asking stupid questions. A jerk to the right accompanied by the transport's left wall buckling inward confirmed her fears. They'd been hit. A moment later, the lights went out. In response, Jas's and the units' helmet lights turned on, their beams lighting the impassive faces of their fellows on the opposite bench.

A gasp came through from the pilot's voice-activated

comm. The transport heaved around, and the floor buckled against Jas's feet. She lifted up her legs and told the defense units to do the same. The pilot cried out, there was a thump, and suddenly they were tumbling over and over. Another hit punched straight through the cabin, blasting two units to pieces. Jas felt the tug of depressurization as the air poured out of the ship.

The final hit corrected their spin somewhat, and now the transport lazily turned, powerless and drifting. The hard light of bright stars shone through the holes on either side of the cabin. The air was filled with tiny pieces of what remained of the two destroyed androids, which followed the spinning motion.

"Pilot?" Jas asked. No reply came. She asked again, several times, but he didn't respond.

"Transport 17," she said, hoping the ship's computer would respond to the simple request. She didn't know if she had the authority to use it.

"Yes, Corporal Harrington?"

A sigh of relief passed through her half-open lips. "What's the pilot's status?"

"The pilot is exhibiting no life signs."

Krat.

"How about the ship's engine?"

"The ship's engine received two hits. The second hit penetrated its plating and disabled it."

As the transport made another turn, Jas caught a glimpse of what looked like a far-distant starship, or at least a small area of starship-shaped space that was black among the shimmering sheet of stars. The *Infineon*? Probably, but they had no way of getting there. A jet of light like a falling star streamed past them toward the patch of darkness. As it hit, the light split and spread out, outlining the shape. It was a starship. No doubt about it. And its force field had just repelled a direct hit.

"Transport 17, please hail the Unity destroyer, *Infineon*."

"I'm sorry, Corporal Harrington. My ship-to-ship comm is not working."

The enemy seemed to have stopped firing at them and had returned its fire to the starship, probably correctly judging the transport to be disabled. Without a pilot, Jas and the defense units would spin forever unless an attempt was made to rescue them, and she thought that unlikely, even if someone had noticed the transport appear out of its jump before it was attacked. With their engines dead and their vessel sitting in an area of space hot with the trails left by energy weapons, they would soon be just about impossible to find. She would only last a few weeks, but the units might continue functioning for centuries.

The transport made another circuit of its slow spin, but its motion was still reacting to its final hit. Jas found it had turned slightly so that she could no longer see the *Infineon*, if that was what the starship was. Now, only the white points of distant suns showed through the holes in the transport. Floating gently against her safety harness, Jas wondered if any of them were the suns of planets she'd visited.

She hated the idea of giving up hope, but the chances of a change in their circumstances seemed slim. She didn't fear death, though dying of thirst—which seemed the thing most likely to kill her in her powered armored suit with its limited water supply—wouldn't be pleasant. But thoughts that she would never have the opportunity to set Carl straight on what he'd meant to her, and that she'd never see him, or Sayen, Phelan, Erielle, or Makey again—these thoughts made her sad.

"Corporal Harrington, permission to speak," said one of

the defense units. Jas lifted her eyebrows in surprise. She'd rarely known a unit speak without being spoken to. Her visor display told her it was Pint-Size.

"Permission granted," she replied.

"What is our status, ma'am?"

"Our status is..." Stranded? Waiting to die? "...awaiting further orders."

"Corporal Harrington, our transport's engine is no longer functioning."

"That's correct, LK29."

"Would it be beneficial to our mission if the engine were repaired?"

"Yeahhhh...it would." Jas's stomach clenched. "Are you telling me you can repair it?"

"Please wait a moment, ma'am, while I run a systems check with the ship's computer."

She held her breath.

"The engine is not repairable," announced LK29.

Jas exhaled. *Oh well.*

"But we may be able to power the thrusters directly and move our vessel closer to the nearest friendly starship, the *Infineon.*"

Jas had forgotten that defense units were also walking, talking, fighting power packs. She should have remembered the fact because it was unit power that had kept Sayen alive when a ship they'd been on had crashed. Jas had never heard of units powering thrusters, but if Pint-Size was correct, that might save them. The transport already had momentum. All they had to do was exert a little propulsion at the right moment in its spin to reverse their motion away from the *Infineon.*

"You might? Then do it, LK29. Do it."

Five defense units unbuckled themselves from their

safety harnesses and set to work. They opened the access hatch in the floor of the transport and disappeared through it. Jas marveled at the androids' independence and initiative. If she hadn't known it, she would never have guessed they were the same units who'd been wandering around and bumping into each other in the shuttle bay of the *Camaradon* less than a couple of hours previously. They were acting more like soldiers than machines.

Around a minute later, the transport jumped a little. They were doing it. They were powering the thrusters with their own power packs. She didn't know how long it would take, but eventually they should arrive at the *Infineon*. She just hoped it would still be under Unity control by the time they got there.

At each burst of power from the units to the thrusters, the ship's spin was slowly being corrected. The view from the holes in the cabin stabilized, but the new, steady orientation of the ship showed nothing useful to Jas. She had no visual on the starship they were heading toward. Yet she did see more bolts of light speed past the transport. Despite what Yeroch had told her aboard the *Camaradon*, the battle seemed far from won.

LK29's head appeared in the access hatch in the floor. The android clambered out, followed by another.

"Corporal Harrington, our power is nearly exhausted. Permission to substitute fresh units."

"Permission granted," Jas said. "How much—" A violent lurch from the transport snapped her teeth closed and made her bite her tongue. "Ough." She swallowed the hot, metallic blood that leaked into her mouth. *What the krat was that?* At the same time as the lurch, a powerful shock had run through the ship as if something had collided with it.

The units who had been powering the engine were thrown into the others sitting on the benches.

"Units, strap in," Jas said.

The unsecured units struggled upright and clambered onto the bench, fastening their harnesses immediately. There was another heavy bump, and the last unit to emerge from the hatch, who hadn't had time to secure itself, flew across the cabin and out through a hole. The tips of its fingers caught the edge, and it began to pull itself in, but a third thump broke it free, and it spun away into space.

A bolt of light flashed through the holes, illuminating every nook and cranny, every stain and smear in the cabin. They were under attack again. Jas clenched her fists in frustration. A unit was lost, and there wasn't anything she could do about it. They were like passive targets in a vid game, just waiting to be picked off.

The flashes and erratic bumps continued for another few seconds, then suddenly it was all over.

12

The transport was still. Reverberations in the bench and floor told Jas something was locking onto the exit. It opened, and armed suited-up soldiers poured in, passing Jas as they sped to the far side of the cabin. They began checking the units.

One of them kicked a unit's leg and began gesticulating at another who seemed to be the captain. Jas couldn't hear what the soldiers said, but it was clear from their body language that they were frustrated at finding only units inside the transport.

Jas unfastened her harness and floated free. One of the soldiers swung his weapon around and pointed the muzzle at her. She held up her hands, and the officer waved the soldier down and approached her. He grabbed her shoulders and touched his helmet to hers.

"Are you the only person aboard?" he asked, his voice sounding muffled and distant.

"It's just me and twenty-two units," she replied. Her swollen tongue made her voice thick. " Used to be twenty-five."

"Kr—" said the officer as he pulled away. He pointed at the units and thumbed toward the exit, then grabbed Jas's arm and gestured in the same direction.

She joined the soldiers and units as they left the transport. As soon as she passed through the exit, artificial gravity pulled her to the floor. They were inside a large airlock. With some relief Jas saw the name *Infineon* emblazoned on the walls. Soldiers and units crowded in the airlock, and the last to leave the transport sealed its exit.

They waited for the chamber to fill with air. After some moments, a green light shone above the farther exit, and it slid open. Jas lowered her visor and blinked in the strong light, smelling the familiar, slightly sweaty, tang of a starship's interior.

The soldiers pushed past her and the units to leave the airlock. Jas looked around, wondering what she was supposed to do, but everyone seemed to be ignoring her, including the officer who'd spoken to her inside the transport.

"Units, exit the airlock," she instructed, and brought up the rear as the last of them passed into the destroyer.

They were in an equipment room. The soldiers were removing their helmets and stripping down, still acting as though Jas and her units didn't exist. The troops were of several alien species as well as a few humans. Jas went over to the officer before he took off his suit, which was her only way of identifying him. He was human, his dark hair the same length as his short beard.

"Sir, I'm Corporal Harrington, assigned from the *Camaradon*."

The man nodded without meeting her gaze and pushed his suit below his knees before bending down to pull it off his legs. "Got your orders?"

"No, I was just told to bring these units here. We're reinforcements."

"Great. Just great." He turned to his troops. "Back to your stations."

The space troops left, surly and muttering among themselves.

"Sir," Jas said, "is there some kind of problem?"

"You could say that, Corporal Harrington," he replied. "We lost the fighter ships that pushed you to safety. Two good pilots dead. When we saw your transport had its engine shot to pieces, they wanted to be heroes, thinking they were saving troops." He glanced around at the defense units, who were standing still and silent. "We don't have enough pilots. I just hope you and your units are worth it."

The officer hung up his suit. "You can find a ship's uniform over there. When you're ready, report to Commander Torben." He left her alone with her units.

Jas unclipped her helmet and slowly removed it. *Two good pilots dead.* Now she knew why the soldiers had been disappointed and angry to find only defense units aboard the transport.

The bangs and bumps the transport received had been the fighter ships pushing it the remainder of the distance to the ship. Such a maneuver would have taken great skill. Jas's heart froze at the thought that one of the pilots might have been Carl. The enemy must have spotted what was happening and attacked the vulnerable fighters.

"LK29, are you in contact with the *Infineon's* computer?"

"Yes, Corporal Harrington."

"Can you read its data banks? Like, can you find out the names of the pilots on board?"

"I do not have the necessary permissions."

"Okay. Can you tell me where I can find Commander Torben?"

JAS HAD TOLD the units to wait in the equipment room as she didn't know what she was supposed to do with them. She followed Pint-Size's directions through the ship's corridors, heading toward the bridge. The ship was as utilitarian as the transport had been. The metal floor was worn and scuffed with the passage of thousands of booted feet. No signs explained what was down the corridors or behind each door, possibly as a defense against boarders. Jas imagined that the soldiers had to memorize the layout of the ship.

The whine of air filters and the scent of burnt plastic and chemicals told her the ship's force field hadn't been an adequate defense against all the fire targeted at it. A repair bot almost hit her as it flew past on its way to fix something, and at one point she must have been near the ship's hull, for the metal on one side of the corridor was discolored and warped. At the sound of running feet from up ahead, she moved over to allow the approaching soldiers to pass. In another second the group appeared. They were nearly past her when she heard a snippet of dialogue about the fighter ships still in action.

"Hey," exclaimed Jas. "Hey, are you pilots?"

One of the group turned her head. "Yeah. What's it to you?"

"Is there a pilot called Lingiari aboard this ship?"

"No. Leastways, I never heard of him," called the woman, then the group was gone.

Jas finally found the bridge. After the guards had let her

enter, she was a little relieved to see that Commander Torben was a Cruthian, like Flahive had been.

Everyone on the bridge was focused on a hologram that hung in midair in the center. Jas noticed the dark-haired officer who had entered the transport was there. He and the other officers sat at controls around the constantly moving image, which displayed four suns and many dots in a range of colors. This was the area where the Unity and Shadow ships had met head on. One color—red—predominated, and Jas guessed that it signified the enemy ships. The other colors had to be Unity ships of various classes or those belonging to the galactic alliance.

Some of the dots were pulsing and moving slowly, others were still and steady. The red dots of many Shadow ships were motionless. If Jas was reading the hologram correctly, it looked like the Shadow forces had nearly been defeated.

Torben lifted an upper limb to Jas as she approached the commander, its disc-like appendage held flat. Jas paused and awaited the commander's attention.

"Enemy ship on the move in sector six," said an officer, lifting her eyes from her interface to the hologram.

Jas saw it: a pulsing red light was moving slowly in the direction of the nearest sun, as if intending to slip behind the star for protection. Though the ship was crawling, it must have been traveling incredibly fast.

"That's ours," said Torben. "After it before it jumps. Prepare all pulses."

The bridge of the *Infineon* shifted beneath Jas's feet as the artificial gravity took a moment to compensate for the sudden movement of the ship. Jas gazed at the hologram. She'd never seen a space battle before. The blinking green light that crawled toward the Shadow ship had to represent the *Infineon*.

"Pulse distance in forty-three seconds," said another officer.

"If it doesn't jump before we get there," muttered someone else.

"Quiet on the bridge," barked Torben. Though her translator moderated her voice to a near monotone, somehow the feeling behind the words was carried through.

"Corporal Harrington?" Torben asked.

Jas was so intent on the hologram, she almost didn't realize she was being addressed. "Yes, Commander."

"We just received notification of your arrival from the *Camaradon*," Commander Torben said. "A little late. You and your units are to sweep defeated vessels. Remain on standby."

"Yes, Commander," Jas replied, impressed by the commander's coolness in dealing with side business when about to engage in battle. Jas wasn't sure if she should leave. She decided she would stay, at least until Torben noticed she was still there and dismissed her.

"Pulse distance in twenty seconds."

"Prepare to engage," Torben said. The officers at the consoles surrounding the hologram fixed their eyes on the image. Their hands hovered over their interfaces. If the *Infineon* had been in the battle from the start, which had been soon after the Council officers had arrived at Ganymede Outpost, they'd already been fighting for many hours.

"Ten seconds."

The hologram zoomed from a general display of the battle zone to a detailed image containing the *Infineon* and the Shadow ship. Now, the dots moved much faster. The red dot was streaking away from the green one and curving into the outer orbit of the sun. The green dot was gaining on it, however.

The atmosphere in the room became tense.

"Five seconds. Four. Three. Two. One."

Three tiny pale yellow dots sprang from the *Infineon*. They traveled faster than the destroyer, and faster than the enemy ship. The red dot responded with some kind of weapons of its own, laying down a trail of defensive fire, a long line of sparks that ranged behind it.

"Evasive maneuver," Torben said.

The deck dropped from beneath Jas's feet as the *Infineon's* pilot took the ship abruptly downward. She became momentarily airborne and grabbed a rail to steady herself. The ship's artificial gravity didn't seem to be working properly. Maybe it had been damaged in earlier skirmishes. The sparks drew closer.

The enemy ship also attempted a maneuver, abruptly changing its trajectory with a speed that would have tested the ship to the limits of its strength, Jas guessed. But the *Infineon's* pale yellow bolts of energy had just enough time to alter their course to match the change in direction of their target. They sank into the red dot and vanished just before the Shadow ship's sparks converged on the *Infineon*. Many passed them, but the tail hit, and Jas heard and felt their dull thumps on the hull.

The red dot stopped moving. Whoops, hollers, and alien celebratory noises filled the bridge.

"Quiet on the bridge," Torben barked again. "Damage report."

"Force field's down again, Commander," said an officer. "Damage to decks five through seven. Details still arriving. Repair crews dispatched."

"Right. Keep me up to date on the situation."

Another officer said, "Commander, the scanners are

showing we took out the Shadow ship's jump engine. It's going nowhere."

"Excellent. Good work, everyone," said Torben.

"Unity Command is hailing, ma'am," someone else said.

"Thank you," Torben said. "Please ask Command for permission to put the comm on general broadcast."

"Yes, ma'am." A pause. "Permission granted. Routing to ship's comm."

A voice sounded from the bridge intercom. "Crew of the *Infineon*, this is Commander General Coney. Congratulations. You just took out the last Shadow ship remaining in the vicinity."

And with that, all hell broke loose.

13

Torben was the first to die. One of the guards lifted his weapon and calmly blasted the commander in the head. As the Cruthian's suit split apart, her body erupted in a massive froth through the gap. Jas was already running at the guard. He saw her and turned, but before he had a chance to fire his weapon again, she drove her shoulder into his chest, throwing him back against the wall. The impact to his head stunned him, and he slid toward the floor. Jas grabbed his weapon as he fell and turned it upon him. His eyes widened briefly before she burned a hole through his skull.

Fights had broken out all over the bridge as the Shadows attacked the non-Shadow officers. Jas focused on the comm officer who had relayed the Command message. The alien was a large quadruped, and he was sitting frozen, watching the battle around him. Jas killed a Shadow who was aiming at him.

"You," she shouted. "Ship wide alert. Shadows aboard. Shadows aboard. Got it?"

The comm officer withdrew his gaze from the dying

Shadow who had been about to kill him. He fumbled at his interface.

"Wait," said the dark-haired officer as he took out another Shadow who was targeting the quadruped. "Implement Operation Penumbra," he barked at the alien.

The comm officer's mouth quivered.

"Implement Operation Penumbra," the dark-haired officer repeated.

He spun and fired at Jas. She ducked, too late, but the energy bolt passed to her left. As she turned, a Shadow crumpled to the ground behind her. He'd saved her life.

"Implement Operation Penumbra," the comm officer said into his mic and immediately slid under his console. The alien's words were repeated through the bridge intercom and no doubt throughout the ship. Jas threw herself under another desk and found herself sharing a cramped space with the dark-haired officer.

Operation Penumbra. In spite of appearances, the Council's warning had gotten through and the Unity had put some kind of plan in place to respond to a Shadow attack from the inside, though Jas couldn't figure out what it was.

Bolts were still flying around the bridge. When they hit Torben's remains, they hissed through the foam. The white mound was a substantial impediment to straight shooting on the bridge. The surviving combatants had all found shelter and were taking random pot shots at each other. The hologram of the *Infineon* and the Shadow ship in space still hung suspended in midair. From her place of temporary safety, Jas had a good view of the image. The red dot had begun to move swiftly toward the *Infineon*.

"Krat," she muttered.

"What's wrong?" asked the dark-haired officer squashed

in with her. He pushed her to one side as he reached out to take a shot.

"That Shadow ship we hit is heading right for us," said Jas.

The man glanced at the hologram before taking another shot. "Krat indeed. We need to get out of here."

"You said it." Jas elbowed him out of the way to lean out. She'd timed it just right. A Shadow's head appeared. She shot and hit it. The Shadow had fired at the same time, but its bolt went slightly wide and hit the wall of the console they were hiding behind.

"Ahhh," the man yelped as the metal that he was squashed against grew hot. He tried to move away, but there was too little room. They were jammed shoulder to shoulder. Jas tried to give him a few centimeters of space.

"The problem is," he said, wincing, "we don't know who's a Shadow and who isn't."

"I'm pretty sure the ones shooting at us are Shadows," said Jas. "We were protecting the comm officer so he could get the message out, and they were trying to kill him."

"Good point. So how do we kill *them*?"

"We call for reinforcements," said Jas. She lifted her comm button to her lips. "Units to the bridge. We could do with a little help here."

It was Pint-Size who replied. "Affirmative, Corporal Harrington. We're on our way."

"Now we just need to survive the next few minutes," Jas said.

Another energy bolt must have hit the metal panel her shelter companion was crushed against because his face became a mask of pain.

"Here," Jas said, "swap places."

His eyes and lips pressed tightly closed, the man shook

his head. He opened his eyes and reached out to take another shot. "They're on the move," he muttered as he drew himself inside.

Jas took a peek and saw a Shadow run across open space toward the comm officer's station. The Shadow disappeared behind Torben's remains, but Jas had her muzzle trained on the figure, and she shot at where the Shadow was about to be. A heavy thud confirmed the hit.

"Good shot," said the man. His face shone with sweat.

A cry of fear and pain sounded. The man looked out and drew quickly back. "Another one to the Shadows," he said. "And we've lost the hologram."

"Doesn't matter," said Jas. "We know what's happening. We just need to do something about it."

"When we get out of this kratting hole," the officer said. "I just hope we have a live pilot." The ship's pilot had been the first officer the Shadows shot after Torben.

From outside the bridge came shouting and thuds. *Shouldn't be long.* The doors blocked the soft hiss of laser guns, but Jas had little doubt what was happening outside. Her eyes met the officer's as they awaited the outcome of her units' fight with the Shadows.

She peeked out from their hiding place once more and saw the muzzle of a weapon poking out from behind a console, aiming at the bridge door. The Shadow was planning on blasting whoever came through it. Jas ducked back under cover. It would be a difficult shot, but she thought she could do it.

"Cover me," she said to the man, and she leapt out from behind the desk.

He immediately began laying down defensive fire around the room. Jas used the extra second she needed to take careful aim and fired at the weapon muzzle that was targeting the door. The muzzle melted and flamed just as the doors shuddered and gave a metallic groan. A gap appeared between the two halves. The defense units were physically forcing the doors open. The mechanism whined as they pulled them apart.

More Shadows leapt out from their shelters to fire at the defense units. Jas and the dark-haired officer took some of them out, and the units also came through the doors firing.

In less than a minute, the Shadow rebellion on the bridge was finally quelled. Less than a fifth of the officers had been Shadows, but they'd acted immediately when the Unity had seemed on the verge of victory. It had been the same aboard the *Galathea*, Jas reflected. The Shadows had concentrated on replacing those in charge, and those they hadn't managed to replace were the first to die.

The remaining non-Shadow officers emerged from their hiding places, holding up their hands. The comm officer was one of those who had survived the battle, though the quadruped was trembling with shock.

"Back to your stations," said the dark-haired officer. "We're not out of the woods yet."

"The pilots," Jas said to him. "They'll go after the pilots next." She swung around to the units on the bridge. "Go straight to the pilots' quarters and protect them from attack. And bring one here."

14

It was carnage on the bridge. The bodies of Shadows and officers sprawled everywhere, and Torben's remains were slowly collapsing. Several officers had been wounded.

The dark-haired man was talking to the comm officer. As he finished, he turned to Jas and said, "The pilots suffered some casualties too, but they've got the situation under control. One of them is on her way."

"We need to get that holo working," Jas said. The words had hardly left her mouth before the ship shook with a series of explosions. Her ears rang.

"The Shadow ship's firing on us," exclaimed the dark-haired officer. "What's our force field status?"

"Still down, sir," came the reply. "Decks five through seven caught the worst of it again."

"Krat. Where's that holo? Never mind. There's no time. Pulse response, on the double. Evasive maneuv— Krat. Where's that pilot?"

He leaned over the back of another officer to focus on

the interface she was looking at. An impact on the ship threw Jas to the floor, along with everyone else still standing.

"Damage to decks one and two, sir. Hull breach."

The dark-haired officer didn't reply. He glanced at the door, which had buckled where the defense units had forced it open. They needed a pilot. Without the ability to fly, they were sitting ducks.

"Pulses incoming," exclaimed a voice.

"LK29, what's the ETA on that pilot?" Jas said into her comm, but at the same time the female pilot Jas had spoken to earlier ran through the door. Without missing a beat she jumped into the vacant pilot seat. She paused, her hands above the screens on the console. "Hmmm...never flown a destroyer before." She scanned the screens intently. "Let's try..." She swiped a screen and pressed another. "Okay, got it. I see unwelcome visitors. Oh no you don't." She pressed decisively and Jas was crushed to the floor as the ship swept upward incredibly fast.

"More pulses on their way."

"Pilot, emergency jump," said the dark-haired officer from his new position on the floor.

"As quick as I can, sir," the pilot replied.

A deep vibration rose through Jas as the engines began to build power. She started to get up, but another hit buffeted the ship, and she was flung to one side.

"Hull breach deck five." The air was growing hazy with smoke from the damaged areas of the ship. Jas blinked and coughed as the acrid air stung her eyes and throat.

"We scored a hit, sir," said the weapons officer, "but they're still coming."

"Fire with everything we've got," said the dark-haired officer. "Fire at will."

The vibrations grew stronger. Jas had given up trying to stand, deciding that she was safest staying where she was.

"Hold on, everyone," shouted the pilot. The ship rolled and pitched. Jas grabbed the leg of a console. Suddenly the artificial gravity went haywire, and she was hanging suspended in midair, holding on with one arm. The side of the bridge was fifteen meters or so below her. Torben's remains and bodies of dead Shadows and officers had slid and rolled to the bottom. Some of the living were among them, struggling to get away from the corpses.

The pilot and other officers who remained in their seats were hanging precariously to one side. The pilot was trying to fasten her safety harness one-handed. Someone fell and landed heavily on a dead Shadow.

Jas reached up with her left hand to grab the console leg and hold on more securely. Her right hand was already slipping. She missed, grunted, and reached again. But the ship was vibrating so strongly, her fingertips couldn't get a grip. Her shoulder felt like it was being pulled from its socket. For the third time, she swung her left arm up and attempted to grasp the leg. For the third time, she didn't make it.

Her other hand slowly opened as she lost her grip. She was holding on with only her fingers, then they too began to slip. Jas looked down, wondering if she could survive the fall if she landed well. The last of her strength left her fingers, and she dropped like a stone.

When she was halfway down, they jumped.

She never hit the bottom. As they came out of the jump, Jas found herself floating in the center of the bridge. The pilot had shut down the artificial gravity as they'd jumped. The other officers were also suspended in midair or in seats, hastily fastening their safety harnesses.

"Position report, pilot," said the dark-haired officer. He was floating, trying to hook a foot under a chair arm.

"Just a minute, sir." The woman scanned her interface.

"You mean you don't know where we've jumped to?"

"No navigator to figure it out, sir. Had to take a chance."

"Krat, Pilot Kennewell, we could've ended up in the middle of a star."

"Well, the chances of that are—"

"Do not answer me back, madam," the officer barked. "You took an unacceptable risk with the lives of my crew. I shall consider your behavior for a formal reprimand."

The already-quiet bridge grew quieter still as even the wounded officers' groans momentarily quietened.

Jas felt for the pilot. As far as she could tell, the woman had saved all their lives. She wondered if the dark-haired officer was just feeling the stress and responsibility of his new command or if he was always a misborn.

After a pause, the pilot said, "Yes, sir."

15

It turned out that they were only a few light years from the scene of the battle. The engines hadn't generated sufficient power in the short time available to take them very far, but they had escaped the notice of the Shadows, for the time being.

The dark-haired officer asked for ship-wide status reports, and the ship's crew listed the dead and injured along with the material damage to the ship. As that went on, someone must have been fixing the artificial gravity because, not long after the last of the reports came in, and when it was established that all the surviving crew had gotten themselves to a safe place, the gravity reactivated.

Jas had propelled herself into an unoccupied seat on the bridge. She welcomed the return of the sensation of heaviness. She couldn't remember the last time she'd slept properly. She felt beyond exhausted and would have given a lot to close her eyes there and then and rest just for a little while. But there was still plenty of work to be done.

The dark-haired officer was in one-to-one comm with

Unity Command, and the uninjured officers began the clean-up. Jas ordered the units to help with taking the wounded officers to the medical bay, but another officer intervened and said that a better use of the androids would be helping the repair crews to seal the hull breaches. She changed her order and sent them to the relevant decks before lending a hand to carry out the wounded officers herself.

The medical bay was already full of injured crew members, and the medics were busily triaging every man, woman, and alien who went in. Jas left them to it and returned to the bridge to help with the more gruesome task of removing the corpses.

By the time she returned, however, the dead bodies were already gone and some kind of order had been established. The dark-haired officer was still bent intently over the comm panel, speaking quietly into his mic. The quadruped had finally stopped trembling.

Technicians were running diagnostics on controls, though more than half of the stations were empty. Everyone seemed busy except Pilot Kennewell. She was resting her chin on her hand and staring glumly into an interface.

"*I* thought you did a great job," Jas said, taking an adjacent seat.

The pilot sat up and glanced at the dark-haired officer. "Better watch your words around Pacheco," she said quietly. "Or he'll consider you for a formal reprimand too." She rolled her eyes. "Hey, wasn't it you who was looking for someone earlier?"

"Yeah. He's a pilot. Carl Lingiari. Have you heard of him? He joined the battle late."

"No. I'm sorry. He must be on another ship."

"I thought so." Jas was disappointed to find him not

aboard, but also relieved to confirm that Carl couldn't have been one of the pilots who'd been killed rescuing her and the units.

"You're new, aren't you?" asked Kennewell.

"Yeah, I only arrived from the *Camaradon* a little while ago. Just before the final attack."

"Oh, you're the…" Kennewell's eyes widened.

"Yep. I was the one aboard the transport two pilots died saving." She looked down.

"Hey," said Kennewell, "don't feel bad about it. We all knew the risks when we signed up, and the pilots who brought you to safety volunteered for the job. No one ordered them to do it, and if they hadn't, I wouldn't be sitting here now."

In response to Jas's puzzled frown, she went on, "Your units killed the Shadow pilots who were in the process of picking off the rest of us. If those pilots who died hadn't saved your units, they wouldn't turned up to save *us*, I wouldn't have been around to fly us out of trouble."

"What about Operation Penumbra?" Jas asked. "Wasn't that a response plan?"

"It was, but we only had a few hours to work on it. Commander Torben had begun screening everyone to find out if we had any Shadows aboard, but it had to be done secretly so as not to let the Shadows know that we suspected they were among us. We were also in the middle of a battle. Everyone who passed the screening was armed and warned of the danger. Operation Penumbra was the code sign to let us know that the Shadow rebellion had begun and we were to watch for attacks, defend ourselves, and stun and confine anyone we suspected of being a Shadow. But it was too little, too late."

Pacheco straightened up and took off his earpiece and

mic. "Okay, listen up," he said, his tone sharp. The man looked weary, and he had to be in a lot of pain from the burn he'd sustained while he'd been hiding with Jas.

"Things aren't looking too good right now. We lost three ships to the Shadows during that attack from within, which makes seven altogether when we count the ships destroyed during the battle." He sighed and passed a hand across his face. "Unity Command will send lists of the crews lost as soon as they have them. The Shadow attack turned things around somewhat. The battle's over, but no one's won. As soon as we receive coordinates, we will regroup with the remaining vessels."

He stopped and seemed to have nothing else to say.

After a moment's silence someone said, "And then what, sir?"

Annoyance flickered across Pacheco's face. "What do you think, man? That fight was just a skirmish. Now we begin the war."

How long Jas had known that it would come to this, she couldn't remember, but Pacheco's words were no surprise to her. The Shadows were an infestation that, each time you thought you had vanquished them, they would reappear in another place, more numerous and deadlier. Their great strength was their replication of their victims. They could hide in plain sight as the colleagues, friends, family, and lovers of every sentient being they replaced, biding their time until the moment was ripe to rise up and take over.

Jas didn't know how they could stop them, or if they could ever be stopped. The war had only just started and it could be years before it was finally over. She was separated from Carl and from her friends, and she was caught up in the conflict with no end in sight.

All she could do was continue to fight their deadly enemy and hope that, one day, she might be reunited with the people she loved.